Samuel French Acting Edition

Wipe Away
by Mark Snyder

SAMUELFRENCH.COM   SAMUELFRENCH.CO.UK

FOR PRODUCTION ENQUIRIES

UNITED STATES AND CANADA
Info@SamuelFrench.com
1-866-598-8449

UNITED KINGDOM AND EUROPE
Plays@SamuelFrench.co.uk
020-7255-4302

Each title is subject to availability from Samuel French, depending upon
country of performance. Please be aware that *WIPE AWAY* may not be
licensed by Samuel French in your territory. Professional and amateur
producers should contact the nearest Samuel French office or licensing
partner to verify availability.

MUSIC USE NOTE

Licensees are solely responsible for obtaining formal written permission from copyright owners to use copyrighted music in the performance of this play and are strongly cautioned to do so. If no such permission is obtained by the licensee, then the licensee must use only original music that the licensee owns and controls. Licensees are solely responsible and liable for all music clearances and shall indemnify the copyright owners of the play(s) and their licensing agent, Samuel French, against any costs, expenses, losses and liabilities arising from the use of music by licensees. Please contact the appropriate music licensing authority in your territory for the rights to any incidental music.

IMPORTANT BILLING AND CREDIT REQUIREMENTS

If you have obtained performance rights to this title, please refer to your licensing agreement for important billing and credit requirements.

WIPE AWAY received its world premiere production in July 2010 by |the claque| at the 35th Annual Samuel French Off Off Broadway Short Play Festival at the Lion Theatre in New York City. It was directed by Nick Leavens; the production designer was Eric Beauzay; the sound designer was Carl Bishop; the graphic designer was Jason Schroeder; and the production assistant was Alexandra Siladi. The cast was as follows:

TRAVIS. . . . . Thomas Muccioli
GINA. . . . . Jessica Kinsella

Special Thanks: Midori Nohara, Robin Benson, Ryan Smith, Matthew Givens, David J. Castellano, Shaun Sperling, Heather Schmucker, Justin Boyd, Sarah Zettler, Addae Moon, Ryan Glass, and the Ohio Five.

CHARACTERS

TRAVIS – 19, but looks younger
GINA – 18, but looks older

SETTING

The Midwest

TIME

Late summer

To Chantal Bilodeau

(The side of a highway road passing a farmhouse a short distance from a mid-size city in Ohio. The farmhouse is about a quarter mile from the road. A set of mailboxes indicates the surrounding addresses. The sun is just starting to come up in the early twilight of morning. There is a night chill in the air.)

(The headlights from a passing car illuminate **TRAVIS** *standing at the side of the road. He is alert and runs to retrieve his backpack that is hidden by the mailboxes.)*

(The car passes, leaving **TRAVIS** *standing in the dark, waiting. Silence.)*

(Another car passes.)

*(***GINA*** enters. She is pulling a long, dirty wool sweater around herself. Her hair is gummy and askew, and her bright red lipstick is smeared down her chin and across her cheek.)*

GINA. Careful.

(Pause.)

The moss around the sun porch makes those rocks look smooth, but their shadows are sharp. You'll have to lead the way back.

(Pause.)

What a night, hmm?

(Silence.)

Hardly any moon. Can you still see the moon, Travis?

(Nothing.)

Travis? Come on –

TRAVIS. Morning.

GINA. I almost sliced my toe open.

TRAVIS. *(Points.)* Sun's coming up over there –

GINA. Nah, it's still pitch black!

TRAVIS. – Beyond Scriber's Grocery –

GINA. Nobody's gonna see us from all the way over there.

TRAVIS. *(Still pointing.)* Peeking up over the roof, there's a sliver of light.

GINA. Oh. Well, what a morning, then. Hmm?

    (Silence.)

I can barely stand up I'm so zonked –

TRAVIS. Get back to the house.

GINA. *(Smiling.)* You get back to the house.

TRAVIS. Don't you have somewhere you need to be?

GINA. My bed.

TRAVIS. Isn't there somebody waiting for you?

GINA. Nope, I'm closed for the night –

TRAVIS. *Morning!*

GINA. *Morning.*

TRAVIS. Get it right. Jeez.

GINA. I was sitting in my room, all by myself –

TRAVIS. I find that awful hard to believe.

GINA. – And you know what I was picturing? The three of us in the front seat on our way to Niagara Falls, squished in that truck.

TRAVIS. It was a station wagon.

GINA. Packed so tight together our legs were touching.

TRAVIS. You didn't go to Niagara Falls.

GINA. That click-clacking truck!

TRAVIS. We did, Dustin and me, but you weren't there.

GINA. Sure, I –

TRAVIS. It was before you.

GINA. *(Mocking.) Before* me?

TRAVIS. Jeez.

GINA. How am I supposed to remember what happened before me, Travis?

TRAVIS. You just know, I don't know how –

GINA. He makes it sound real nice.

TRAVIS. You always get stories wrong.

GINA. Everything's fuzzy sometimes, and soft like a cotton swab.

(Pause.)

TRAVIS. Dustin wouldn't even drive me down to see the Falls.

GINA. But he took you to a wax museum!

TRAVIS. Yeah, full of statues with chipped faces and missing eyes –

GINA. Maybe they were winking at you.

TRAVIS. – More like black marbles, falling out and rolling away –

GINA. He didn't tell me that part.

TRAVIS. – And he'd change his voice and hide, tried to convince me the statues were talking.

GINA. *(Giggles.)* Really? The look on your little face, I'll bet –

TRAVIS. So it wasn't "real nice."

GINA. What'd the statues ask you?

TRAVIS. He asked me if I'd ever stuck my nose inside a skinned raccoon and would I like to.

GINA. Dustin's so funny.

(Pause.)

TRAVIS. You look ridiculous.

GINA. I didn't wash up yet.

TRAVIS. All that crap running down your face –

GINA. *(Rubbing at her face.)* There just wasn't enough time, okay?

TRAVIS. Line out the door?

GINA. Hardly. Three fellas all night.

TRAVIS. He'll stress over the bills this month.

GINA. Dustin knows what to do.

TRAVIS. You make your face even redder when you wear lipstick.

GINA. I like red. I look okay in red –

TRAVIS. They just smear it all over your face.

GINA. – Don't I, Travis? Don't I look okay in red?

TRAVIS. Red's fine. Here.

(He holds out a handkerchief. She takes it.)

GINA. You keep your stuff so white and clean. I hate to get it dirty.

(Folds the handkerchief carefully.)

So this guy tonight, he paid Dustin double to spend the night? He drove down from Wyoming and he said his name is Hugh. He was –

TRAVIS. "Real nice."

GINA. He was real nice to me! Stop it. He got down on his hands and knees on the floor like a little prairie dog. He was being so cute I rubbed him on the ear!

TRAVIS. I'll bet that's not all you rubbed.

GINA. *(Giggles again.)* Hugh told me about this fruit called an apricot, it's soft and pink and then you bite into it and juice squirts all over –

TRAVIS. He's still on the floor?

GINA. – But then he turned on me, Travis. You know when that happens? He's coming at me with his teeth and he's trying to be all sweet, but what he's actually doing is holding me down on the bedspread so I can't see the handle on the door. Still going on about this apricot. Hugh's really strange.

TRAVIS. You shouldn't try to remember what they say, Gina.

GINA. It stays hazy if I don't. And anyway, he was over with it before I got real uncomfortable. Then he kisses both of my pinkies good night, my Sir Hugh. Could you hear us?

TRAVIS. I wasn't in my room.

GINA. Were you working downstairs? Maybe that's why Hugh chose me.

TRAVIS. You should go on back to the house now, Gina.

(Pause.)

GINA. Dustin can bring you back. Any time he wants to.

TRAVIS. Can you hear yourself?

GINA. You could have helped me tonight. With Hugh.

TRAVIS. I've had an apricot, thanks.

GINA. Hugh said my hugs are better than blankets. You should let me hug you.

(Silence.)

Dustin wouldn't mind.

TRAVIS. Dustin's nothing. He's a teeny speck on the face of the planet.

GINA. Then me and you, we're really nothing I guess. If he's teeny –

TRAVIS. Blink and you'd miss him.

GINA. That's real mean, Travis. Take it back.

TRAVIS. You can't touch me.

GINA. I'll tickle you with crab apple grass!

TRAVIS. You'd still have to catch me first!

GINA. (Giggles.) You're so serious.

TRAVIS. It's the vein popping out of my head. You know the rules about touching.

GINA. Ah, but you never follow the rules.

TRAVIS. I follow this one.

GINA. And it's Dustin's rule, Travis, not ours –

TRAVIS. But you won't go against Dustin, will you?

(Silence.)

GINA. Hey, the sun *is* coming up through those trees. Have you ever seen anything so fantastically wiggy as that?

TRAVIS. Nobody gets these sunrises in a city.

GINA. Dustin says we're charmed.

TRAVIS. Don't bring him out here, Gina.

GINA. You know, some of us kind of enjoy Dustin's company from time to time! Maybe he'd like to see this sunrise with us.

TRAVIS. I'll be gone before he gets out the door.

GINA. You belong here.

TRAVIS. I can't "belong" anywhere.

GINA. You like it here. You do.

TRAVIS. You're delirious from lack of sleep.

GINA. And you can't tell me you don't, not with a straight forehead!

(GINA nudges TRAVIS in the back.)

TRAVIS. Don't.

GINA. And the other kids –

TRAVIS. Screeching little chimps.

GINA. – Tommy walks around imitating you, and Simone has this crush that's not going away. I think she's jealous of me.

(GINA nudges again. TRAVIS pulls away.)

TRAVIS. Just knock it off, okay?

GINA. The twins get to climb all over you.

TRAVIS. The *twins* – don't work upstairs yet!

GINA. So if I came downstairs, worked downstairs, I'd be allowed – ?

TRAVIS. Doesn't that bother you, Gina? All those rules –

GINA. Every family has rules.

TRAVIS. Every family.

GINA. Sure, like washing our hands before dinner.

TRAVIS. Using bleach and not soap?

GINA. So Dustin likes to know they're clean.

TRAVIS. Don't you ever stop to think about why we have to follow all these rules, just so we can live all the way out here? With him?

GINA. Sure.

TRAVIS. And what do you come up with?

GINA. Um.

TRAVIS. How does it make you feel?

GINA. Exhausted.

TRAVIS. I mean it. Dustin's not right. He's a freak.

GINA. Travis, no!

TRAVIS. Don't you just want to get away from here and find normal people?

>   *(Silence.* **GINA** *giggles.)*

GINA. We're supposed to laugh at you, Travis.

TRAVIS. Like a jack-in-the-box. Wind me up and out I pop.

GINA. Dustin says that's your best thing. You being so funny.

TRAVIS. He doesn't even crack a smile at what I say.

GINA. He laughs behind his teeth.

TRAVIS. *(Smiles.)* See? You can be the funny one from now on. The kids will be fine.

>   *(Pause.)*

GINA. I don't like this anymore.

TRAVIS. I'm leaving, Gina.

GINA. Yeah, you sound like you actually think you really are going to get away. It's odd.

TRAVIS. Maybe it's easier if you just laugh at me.

>   *(***GINA*** *giggles.)*

Go on, laugh all the way back to the house.

>   *(***GINA*** *keeps laughing as he stares at her. She abruptly stops.)*

GINA. You smell Dustin's t-shirts after he wears them. I've seen you.

TRAVIS. Shuddup. He watches me get ready, like he's not quite sure how to do it himself.

GINA. He likes watching you do stuff. You're elegant.

TRAVIS. Nobody's ever called me that before Dustin.

GINA. See? He cares about you.

TRAVIS. Yeah, he cares how much I can bring in every night.

GINA. It's not like that.

TRAVIS. Wait until I'm gone.

GINA. He'll be really sad, he won't think about money. Dustin loves you, Travis.

(**GINA** *touches* **TRAVIS** *again, lightly.*)

TRAVIS. Every other word out of your mouth is "Dustin"! It's so retarded.

GINA. He looks out for us. The fellas come for us, not Dustin! He needs us so that he can feel part of it.

TRAVIS. Who do you think invites them all up here, those fellas?

GINA. He doesn't have to invite them. They find us.

TRAVIS. But you never wonder how they just know to park their cars alongside the driveway and walk up to the house?

GINA. Most of these fellas are really smart. Accomplished.

TRAVIS. Yeah, how do they know whose name to ask for when they ring the bell?

GINA. Dustin says you're ready to start running a night or two on your own. If you want.

TRAVIS. You're lying.

GINA. He's gonna try you out.

TRAVIS. He really said that?

GINA. Uh-huh.

(*Silence.*)

I'm gonna press your shirts like Dustin's so you look mature and in charge. Starch your collars.

TRAVIS. They'd ask for me.

GINA. Yeah, maybe they'd even notice the fuzz you're trying to grow on your upper lip there!

TRAVIS. Okay, I will tell you something.

GINA. Ooh, what?

TRAVIS. Just – it's really nothing –

GINA. A secret?

TRAVIS. A fact.

GINA. Tell me!

TRAVIS. I snuck out tonight because I didn't want to have to say goodbye to you. I knew it would be tough.

GINA. Really?

TRAVIS. Yes.

GINA. No fingers crossed behind your back?

TRAVIS. You've been my only friend, Gina.

GINA. *Really?* You never act like it.

TRAVIS. I try to be sneaky.

GINA. Keeping your head down all the time, correcting me, never being silly with us anymore –

TRAVIS. I'm laughing behind my teeth.

GINA. See? You *are* ready to be in charge.

(**GINA** *reaches to embrace him.*)

TRAVIS. I'm late.

GINA. You don't have time for a hug?

TRAVIS. I've seen you give one of your hugs. They're quite involved.

GINA. *(Giggles.)* You're right, they are!

(**TRAVIS** *picks up his backpack from behind the mailboxes.*)

TRAVIS. Just think about breaking the rules yourself, okay?

GINA. Where did that come from?

TRAVIS. It's my stuff.

GINA. What stuff?

TRAVIS. Just my own stuff, okay?

GINA. You don't have any stuff. It's all either Dustin's or everybody's.

TRAVIS. Gina.

GINA. What did you steal of mine?

TRAVIS. You should go and check.

GINA. Where are you gonna go?

TRAVIS. I have a ride.

GINA. Here I am, talking like you're actually going to leave –

TRAVIS. Someone's picking me up.

GINA. He wishes he had your face.

TRAVIS. Gina, this could be the last time we ever –

GINA. Dustin can charge three times as much for you as any of the rest of us, and nobody bats an eye as they pay –!

TRAVIS. Can we please stop talking about Dustin!

GINA. He says we're gonna have a turnstile installed at the foot of your bed, so we can keep a tally.

TRAVIS. Nobody touches me.

GINA. Yeah, but you're a talker. They love talking to you. Sometimes that's all they want.

TRAVIS. Exactly.

GINA. I wish I could talk good too, but Dustin says I babble too much, so I have to do more.

TRAVIS. Gina, you just need to stop all the giggling. It makes them nervous – Go back to the house! PLEASE!

GINA. I can get you so crazy sometimes.

TRAVIS. You are better than this, better than him.

GINA. I mean, I can get you mad crazy.

TRAVIS. Just keep your eyes open. Think.

(GINA *pounces on the backpack.*)

GINA. Let's see what you've got in here –

TRAVIS. Gina! LET GO!

(*They struggle with the backpack.*)

GINA. That's our stuff, you can't just walk off with the vases or the pot holders –

TRAVIS. *(Simultaneously.)* This isn't going to get me to stay, you can't make me STAY!

> (**TRAVIS** *grabs* **GINA** *by the arm and pushes her away from the pack.*)

You won't live here forever, Gina.

GINA. This is my family.

TRAVIS. No, your family is the one you went home with from the hospital, when you were born! You didn't come with us until you were seven! Do you remember that? I do.

GINA. I'm better off with Dustin.

TRAVIS. But you were somebody's little girl before this. You can't just forget her!

> *(Pause.* **GINA** *holds her arm.)*

GINA. You hurt me.

TRAVIS. I'm sorry I grabbed you.

GINA. *(Cries.)* OH! Oh no –

TRAVIS. Oh jeez. Let me see.

GINA. My arm's turning purple, the shape of your freakin' thumb on my arm!

TRAVIS. It's dirt from the porch.

GINA. I can't hide bruises! What am I gonna do?

TRAVIS. It's not a bruise. You're just dirty.

GINA. Guys check, they don't pay as much if I have bruises.

TRAVIS. Gimme that handkerchief.

GINA. What, now you have some new magical power? Presto chango and my arm is brand new?

TRAVIS. Hold still.

> *(Wets the handkerchief with spit and wipes her arm.)*

It's my rule, the no touching. I brought you a bouquet of poison ivy into the house that I thought were flowers.

> *(Cleans her face, wiping the lipstick off.)*

TRAVIS. *(Cont.)* And then when I tried to play connect the blisters on your skin using a magic marker, I got it too. Then I gave it back to you, then you gave it to Dustin. So. No more touching.

> *(Pause.)*

We're each our own farmland out here. Side by side with these wire fences around us. It's time to take mine down.

> *(He's done, yet his hand lingers on her cheek.)*

I'm glad you're waiting with me.

> (**TRAVIS** *refolds the handkerchief.*)

GINA. Travis, that's one of Dustin's handkerchiefs.

TRAVIS. It's mine.

GINA. I embroidered the edges with the pale blue thread for his birthday.

TRAVIS. You must have put it in my drawer by mistake.

GINA. You'll think of him every time you blow your nose. HONK!

TRAVIS. I guess it fell into my bag.

GINA. So give it back to me –

> (**TRAVIS** *stuffs it in his pack.*)

– Or not.

> (**TRAVIS** *hoists the backpack on his shoulder, looks down the street.*)

I hear the Rocky Mountains are the highest place in the whole country. You going there?

TRAVIS. Maybe.

GINA. What about Louisiana, New Orleans or Arizona – ?

TRAVIS. How do you know those places?

GINA. We have a globe.

TRAVIS. Yeah, it wouldn't fit in my pack.

> (**GINA** *giggles.*)

No we have plans.

GINA. We?

TRAVIS. His name is Raymond. He's uh got long bushy hair that covers his eyes, and his nose, he broke his nose in a fist fight over a girl in high school. He's been to high school, Gina! And now he wants to start a vineyard in a place called Sonoma. We've got a friend out there who's working at a wine store –

GINA. I thought I was your only friend!

TRAVIS. *Ray's* friend. He's gonna help us. But Ray's smart. He asked me all these questions, like he really wanted to know about me, and I didn't think I would have much to say, but – we broke the same finger when we were both fourteen years old! The left index. Remember?

GINA. Yeah. Sorry.

TRAVIS. He wears jeans with holes in them, and the hair on his leg pokes out.

GINA. I've seen that guy. Dustin says he's got this crazy disease you can't see and drives out here because nobody will talk to him in town.

TRAVIS. Sounds nothing like my guy.

GINA. And Dustin overheard him once at the pharmacy ordering some kind of special skin cream.

TRAVIS. You don't know right from Dustin, do you?

GINA. I'm just telling you what he told me about your friend.

TRAVIS. Well, do you believe him or me?

GINA. Who cares what I think. Do what you want.

TRAVIS. Maybe you just never learned how to form an independent opinion for yourself.

GINA. Don't look at me like that.

TRAVIS. Like what?

GINA. Like you're sorry for me.

TRAVIS. So what do you believe?

GINA. This Ray will leave you in the middle of South Dakota! He'll drive away while you're in the bathroom. You know how that will feel.

TRAVIS. I have to try with Ray! At least I have to try.

>   (*Pause.*)

Did you know that Dustin found me underneath a picnic bench in a state park? They left me there.

GINA. And you knew when you went with him, when he picked you up and took your hand, that it would be better with him, that he'd be kinder to you than they were.

TRAVIS. Is that what he told you?

GINA. Aunt Melanie forgot me in a shoe store at the mall.

TRAVIS. Gina, come with us.

GINA. You and Dustin?

TRAVIS. Come with Ray and me.

GINA. Winter's coming. There's snow to shovel, and since you'll be gone –

TRAVIS. My world's always felt the size of that picnic table, sitting on the ground looking up at the wood bottom. But when I come out here, and I stretch my arms up to the sky and pick out those factories out on the horizon puffing smoke, I see how big our lives could be. It will happen to you too.

GINA. Nah, this is enough for me. Dustin's –

TRAVIS. He knows this is supposed to happen, Gina. He's not gonna be broken up about it. He wants to see if I can survive out there as much as I do. As much as you could.

GINA. I have a shelf for my products in the bathroom near the mirror. You may be feeling disloyal to Dustin right about now, but –

TRAVIS. He's not going to love you the same way he loves –

>   (*Suddenly both are illuminated by another passing car.*)

>   (**GINA** *grabs on to* **TRAVIS**, *practically tackling him to the ground.*)

(The car passes once again.)

Let go.

GINA. You smell like the dryer.

TRAVIS. Please.

GINA. Isn't this nice too? Don't you feel so nice?

TRAVIS. Let me go.

GINA. He touches me, you know, right here on my cheek with his thumb. He never touches anyone else there but me, he told me so, it's our special place. And every time, Dustin tells me I'm not meant to be with just one person, that I'm meant for many. I'm meant to inspire every fella who meets me in that room upstairs. He calls me their best dream.

TRAVIS. He's right.

GINA. Why would I leave someone who says that to me? I'll bet he's all wrapped up and cozy in his bed. His feet all warm under the blankets –

TRAVIS. His bed is cold, Gina.

GINA. – Hmm?

TRAVIS. And empty.

> *(**GINA** giggles.)*

He doesn't sleep there, Gina. You should know that before I go.

GINA. So where does Dustin sleep? Is he a bat?!

> *(Another car. **TRAVIS** starts for the road. **GINA** grabs his arm.)*

NO! Where does Dustin sleep, Travis?

> *(The car passes. **TRAVIS**' shoulders slump.)*

TRAVIS. Ray talks out of the side of his mouth. He'll make you laugh.

GINA. Why are you trying to mix me up?!

TRAVIS. We'll listen to the radio and sing along.

GINA. Where does he sleep if he's not in his bed, Travis?

TRAVIS. Dustin strokes other cheeks, Gina.

GINA. He doesn't touch you.

TRAVIS. And when my thumb is in his mouth and he's holding my mouth closed so we don't laugh at each other, he bites down because he knows I like that –

GINA. We're not supposed to touch! That's the rules!

TRAVIS. YOU ASKED WHERE HE SLEPT! You asked.

>   *(Pause.)*

Don't you get it? I see him and his rules and this house for what it is, because that's what he allowed me to see! He let me start coming out here, giving me chores to do outside. He let me start thinking for myself. Dustin is doing this as much as I am! He needs me to go with Ray.

GINA. So who do I go with?

TRAVIS. I can't help you with that.

GINA. Then just get the hell out of here, Travis! Go! But I'm going back to that house, and I'm going to rip this sweater off and I'm going to *fuck* him, Travis! I'm going to fuck him and kiss him and hug him and make him do exactly what he does to you, because you're no better than me! You aren't!

TRAVIS. You're right, I'm not!

GINA. So why did he choose you?

TRAVIS. Forget him. Come with us!

GINA. But. Why aren't we laughing? Who's going to keep me laughing if you go away? How am I going to remember stuff if you don't make me want to? Were you ever happy here, Travis?

TRAVIS. *(Eyes on the road.)* Where is Ray?

GINA. With us? Were you, Travis?

TRAVIS. He promised.

GINA. Tell me. PLEASE!

TRAVIS. He re-seeded the yard a few years back, remember? So we had sprinklers going all over the grass, turning it green. I'd stare at those jets of water for hours. We caught lightning bugs together when it got dark.

Dustin gave me a glass jar with holes poked through the lid so they could breathe and I taped their names on the bottom. And when Dustin took me to the beach oncc just so we could make a sand castle. Then we sat there until it washed away. When we were normal-like, I was happy.

> *(Another car pulls up. They freeze in the light. The headlights flicker. It's Ray)*

Gina –

GINA. I don't remember any of that.

TRAVIS. But you were there.

GINA. I was?

TRAVIS. Always.

> *(Grabs her in his arms, kissing her forehead.)*

Be good.

> *(**TRAVIS** starts off and **GINA** grabs his pack.)*

GINA. Travis, NO! Can't you just – I'll forget! I'll forget it ALL!

TRAVIS. *(Simultaneous.)* LET ME GO!

> *(**TRAVIS** releases the pack. **GINA** clutches it to her.)*

(Smiles.) Thank you.

GINA. NO!

> *(**TRAVIS** runs for the car.)*

Travis! STOP DOING THIS! Stop kidding around –

> *(We hear the door of the car open and close.)*

I don't care what you do. I'm gonna do what I want, same as you! Same as –

> *(The headlights fade as the car drives away.)*

NO! TRAVIS! You can't – WAIT! Please wait –!

> *(The sun has come up.)*

End of Play